P9-DYY-249

The Most Beautiful Kite in the World

For my father, who made my first kite

—Andrea

For Fasten the Stefman and Limey Rottten

—Leslie

Published in Canada by Fitzhenry & Whiteside,
195 Allstate Parkway, Markham, Ontario L3R 4T8

Published in the United States by Fitzhenry & Whiteside,
121 Harvard Avenue, Suite 2, Allston, Massachusetts 02134

www.fitzhenry.ca godwit@fitzhenry.ca

10 9 8 7 6 5 4 3 2 1

National Library of Canada Cataloguing in Publication
Spalding, Andrea
The most beautiful kite in the world / by Andrea Spalding ;
illustrated by Leslie Elizabeth Watts.
ISBN 1-55041-716-9 (bound).--ISBN 1-55041-805-X (pbk.)
I. Watts, Leslie Elizabeth, 1961- II. Title.
PS8587.P213M6 2003 jC813'.54 C2002-905305-6
PZ7

U.S. Publisher Cataloging-in-Publication Data
(Library of Congress Standards)

Spalding, Andrea.
The most beautiful kite in the world / by Andrea Spalding ;
illustrated by Leslie Elizabeth Watts.-- 1st ed.
[32] p. : col. Ill. ; cm.
Includes index.
Summary: A father and daughter story where a little girl
discovers the magic of kites.
ISBN 1-550471-716-9
ISBN 1-550471-805-X (pbk.)
1. Fathers and daughters – Fiction — Juvenile literature.
2. Kites – Fiction – Juvenile
literature. (1. Fathers and daughters — Fiction. 2. Kites – Fiction.)
I. Watts, Leslie
Elizabeth. II. Title.
[E] 21 PZ7S6353M67 2003

Fitzhenry & Whiteside acknowledges with thanks the Canada Council for the Arts, the Government of Canada through the Book Publishing Industry Development Program (BPIDP), and the Ontario Arts Council for their support for our publishing program.

Design by Wycliffe Smith Design Inc.
Printed in Hong Kong

The Most Beautiful Kite in the World

BY ANDREA SPALDING
ILLUSTRATED BY LESLIE WATTS

Fitzhenry & Whiteside

Jenny ran down the road. If she ran fast enough she would have one whole minute to spend inside the general store. One whole minute to look at the most beautiful kite in the world.

"Excuse me, how much is the beautiful, big kite?" she asked the storekeeper.

"Nine dollars and ninety-five cents," he answered.

Jenny frowned. She only had two dollars and twenty-three cents in her piggy bank, but tomorrow was her birthday. Maybe her father would buy her the kite as a present.

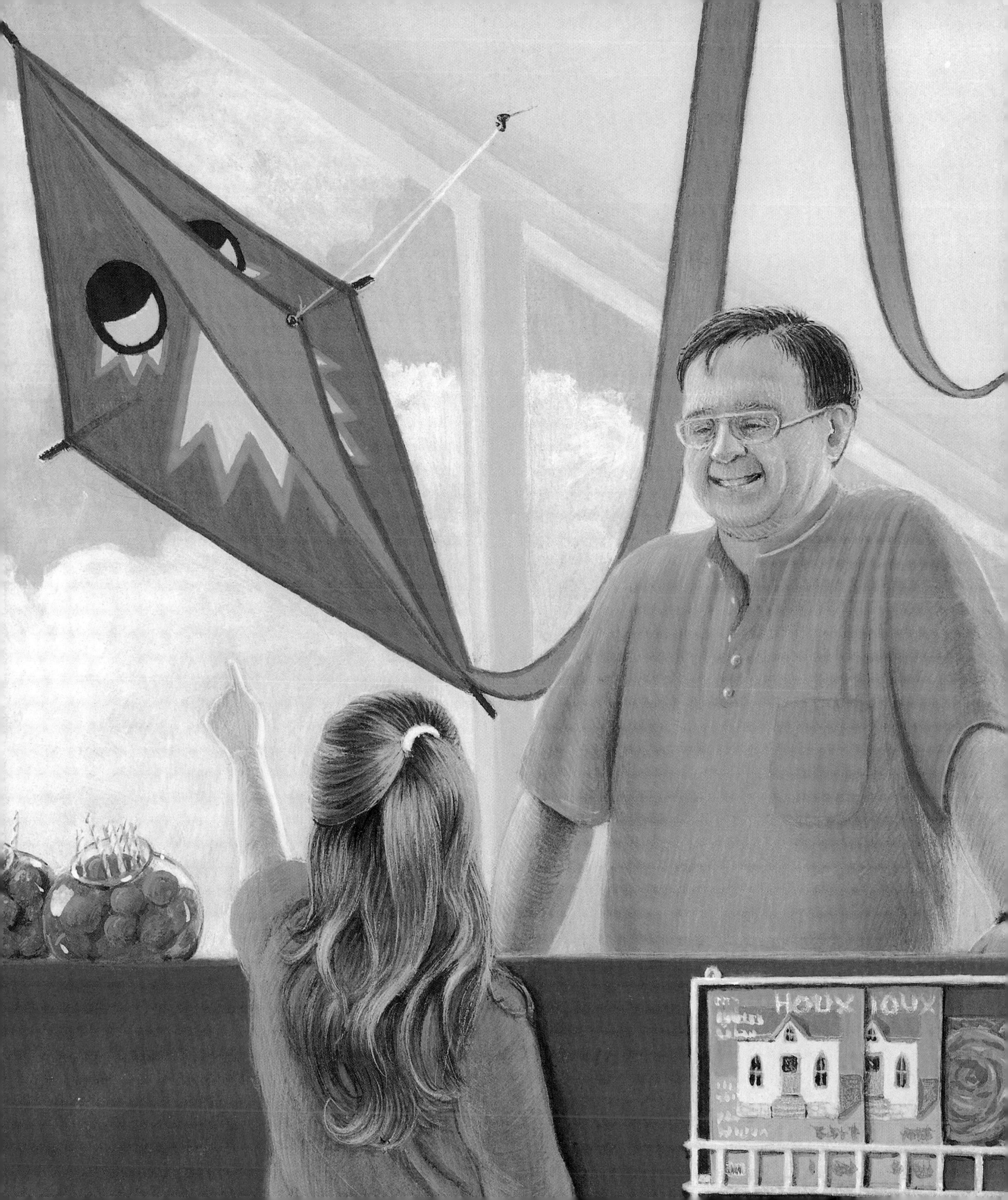
HOUX

The school bell rang, and Jenny skipped carefully down the sidewalk, avoiding all the cracks and humming to herself.

"Step on a crack
Break your back
Take a hike
Fly a kite."

That night, Jenny fell asleep with all
her fingers and toes crossed.

She dreamed of a kite that trailed sunbeams
and flew her to strange, far-off places,
full of balloons and butterflies,
heaving seas and pirate ships.

Jenny's birthday dawned, golden and gusty. Perfect kite weather, she thought.

She jumped out of bed, hurriedly dressed, and ran into the kitchen. There was a kite-shaped parcel by her breakfast bowl. Jenny ripped off the wrapping paper in long strips.

It was a kite. But not the beautiful one from the store. This was a homemade one. She recognized the light wood from her father's workshop. He must have worked while she was asleep, shaping the frame and covering it with white paper.

Jenny's throat felt tight and dry.

"Like it?" her father said.

Jenny smiled but her throat hurt too much to speak. Instead, she ran over and gave him a big, hard hug.

"Eat your breakfast," he said happily, "and we'll go out and see how your kite flies."

The food stuck in Jenny's mouth. She only nodded.

They walked out into the spring sunshine. Her father had a bounce in his step, but Jenny's feet felt like lead and her eyes watered.

"It's the dust," she explained.

Her father took a roll of string from his pocket and helped Jenny attach it to her kite.

"I'll hold the kite while you let out the string," he instructed. "Then, when I shout, run into the wind."

Jenny waited until he carried the kite several paces away and held it up to the breeze.

"Ready, Jenny? Run!"

Jenny ran. But the kite only swooped and dragged in the prairie grass. She sighed with disappointment.

"Hmm," said her father. "That's what I need to know.

It's nose heavy, needs a tail." He tied a loose piece of string to the bottom of the kite.

"Look around, Jenny. See if you can find anything to make bows for the tail."

Jenny scuffed her shoes in the dirt. Why should the kite need bows and a tail? she thought. The beautiful kite would have flown perfectly the first time.

On a nearby porch sat their neighbor, knitting in the sunshine.

Jenny walked slowly over. “Mrs. Omelchuck, please, could you spare me some wool? I need to tie bows on the tail of my kite.”

Mrs. Omelchuck gave her a big, yellow handful.

Jenny took it to her father and stood back to watch him tie three bows that gleamed like sunbeams.

That will never work, she thought disgustedly.

"Come on, Jenny. Let's try again." Her father held the kite high above his head.

"Are you ready with the string? Run!"

This time Jenny felt the kite lift as she sped into the wind.

She glanced back hopefully.

But a moment later the kite fell to the prairie. It was still nose heavy.

Jenny stamped her foot. "I knew it wouldn't fly. This kite will never fly," she cried in frustration.

Her father came over and placed his arm around her shoulders.

"Sure it will," he reassured her. "We just need more bows to balance it."

"Really?" said Jenny. She looked thoughtfully at the kite. It had flown better the second time, and the wool from Mrs. Omelchuck did look pretty.

Her father smiled and ruffled her hair.

"Yup, that's all. Just two or three more bows—"

"And WHOoooOSH, up it goes!" Jenny laughed. She ran off to find them.

Mr. Braun was reading a magazine. Jenny bounced up to him and cleared her throat. He grinned at her.

"Excuse me, Mr. Braun, but I'm trying to get my kite to fly."

"You need help, *liebchen*?"

"We need bows for the tail, and I thought..." Jenny hesitated. "Do you need the cover from your magazine?"

Mr. Braun pulled off the red cover. "I flew kites when I was little. It was fun."

"Oh, thank you, thank you!"

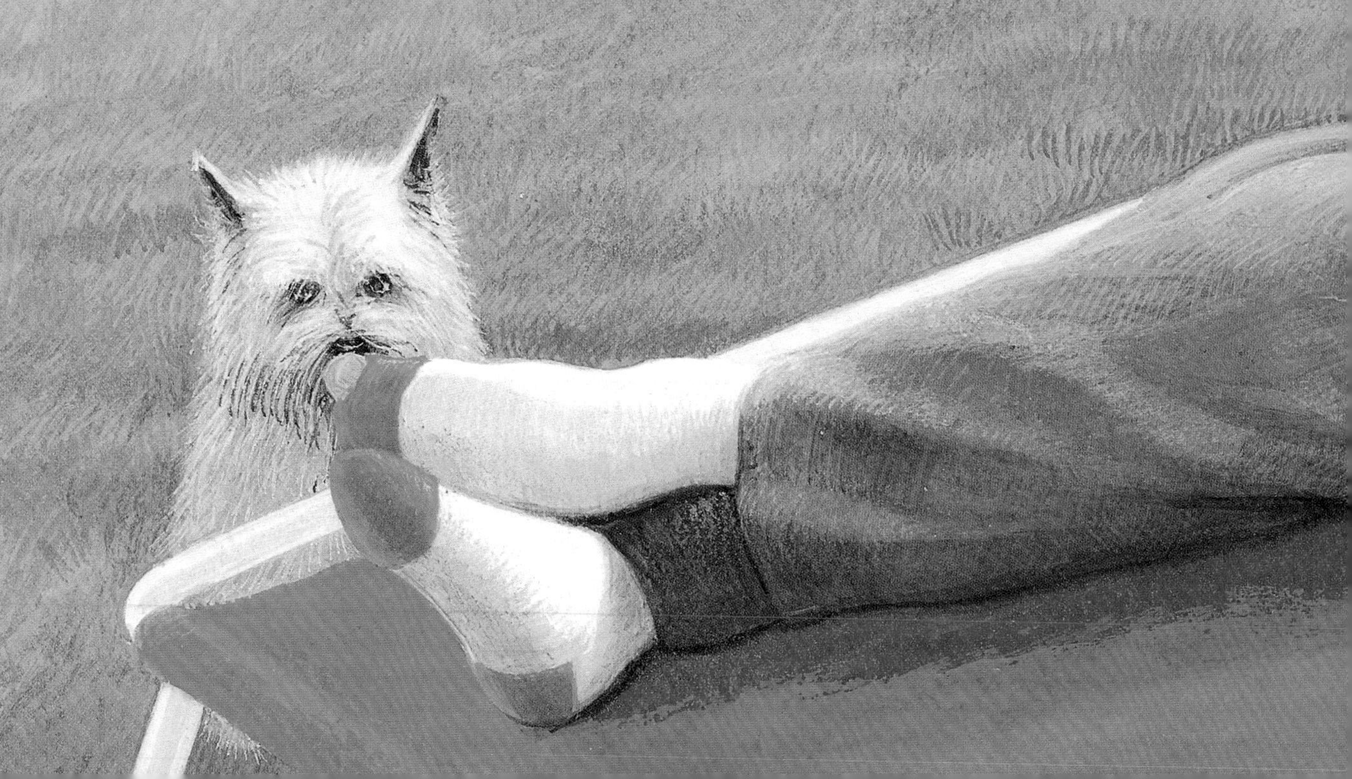

Jenny ran to her father, waving the cover triumphantly.

"Dad, let's try this."

Carefully tearing the paper, they knelt together and added two more bows to the tail.

Once more her father held the kite up.

"Ready, Jenny?"

Jenny nodded eagerly and turned into the wind. She ran, swifter and surer than before. The kite quivered and rose for a minute.

Then the wind dropped, and it fell—SMACK—
to the ground.

"Oh, rats!"

Her father pretended he'd not heard. He picked up the kite and balanced it thoughtfully.

"One more bow should do it."

Jenny looked around. A movement caught her eye. Her friend Charlie was leaning against a truck, peeling a purple wrapper from an all-day sucker.

"Hey, Charlie," she yelled. "Trade you a fly of my kite for that paper off your sucker."

"Doesn't fly yet." Charlie stuck the sucker in his mouth.

"It will if we tie another bow on the tail."

"Well…I guess so." Charlie sauntered over and gave Jenny the purple wrapper.

Jenny tied the purple bow to the tail, handed the kite to her father, and eagerly held the string. Once more he lifted the kite to the breeze.

"One, two, three...NOW!"

Jenny ran. Her feet sped lightly over the grass.

Slowly and uncertainly the kite rose, dipped, then caught the air current and soared upward.

Jenny turned, feeling the kite come alive.

"Quick! Let out more string," called her father.

Jenny carefully unreeled. The kite pulled and climbed and danced.

Jenny grinned an enormous grin.

There above her—soaring, dipping, and playing tag with a meadowlark—was a magical sight.

The early morning sun caught the kite and turned it to dazzling gold. It was Jenny's dream kite! A sunbeam golden kite that swept the sky with a tail of bobbing yellow, red, and purple butterflies.

Around her gathered her father and Charlie, then Mrs. Omelchuck and Mr. Braun. They all looked up in wonder.

"Ooh," they said, "how beautiful."

"Yes," beamed Jenny. "It's the most beautiful kite in the world."

She floated across the prairie with her feet barely touching the earth.

The next day, Jenny flew down the road, past the general store to the school. If she ran fast enough, she would have one whole minute before the bell rang.

One whole minute to show her friends the most beautiful kite in the world.